THIS WALKER BOOK BELONGS TO:

_____

_____

_____

_____

For Tom and Alice with love I.W.

For Alyx with love R.A.

First published 1991 by
Walker Books Ltd, 87 Vauxhall Walk
London SE11 5HJ

This edition published 1993

8 10 9 7

Text © 1991 Ian Whybrow
Illustrations © 1991 Russell Ayto

Printed in Hong Kong / China

British Library Cataloguing in Publication Data
A catalogue record for this book is
available from the British Library.

ISBN 0-7445-3037-7

Quacky quack-quack!

Written by Ian Whybrow

Illustrated by Russell Ayto

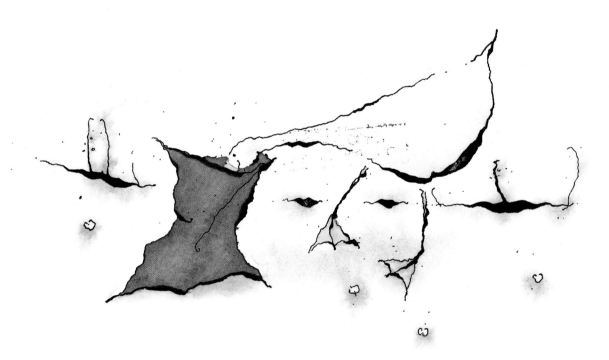

WALKER BOOKS

AND SUBSIDIARIES

LONDON • BOSTON • SYDNEY

This little baby had some bread;
His mummy gave it to him for the ducks,
but he started eating it instead.

Lots of little ducky things
came swimming along,
Thinking it was feeding time,
but they were wrong!

The baby held on to the bag,
he wouldn't let go;
And the crowd of noisy ducky birds
started to grow.
They made a lot of ducky noises…

quacky quack-quack!

Then a whole load of geese swam up
and went *honk! honk!* at the back.

And when a band went marching by,
in gold and red and black,
Nobody could hear the tune –
all they could hear was…

"Louder, boys," said the bandmaster,
"give it a bit more puff."
So the band went toot! toot! ever so loud,
but it still wasn't enough.

Then all over the city, including the city zoo,
all the animals heard the noise
and started making noises too.
All the donkeys went…

ee-aw! ee-aw!

All the dogs went…

WOOf! WOOf!

All the snakes went…

SSSS–SSSS!

All the crocodiles went...

snap! snap!

All the mice went...

squeaky ~ squeaky

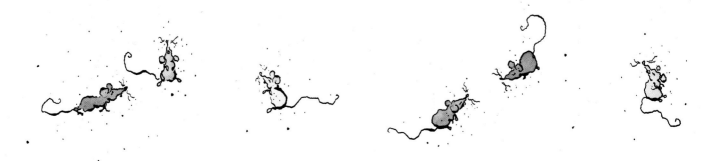

All the lions went...

roar!

Then one little boy piped up and said,
"I know what this is all about.
That's my baby brother with the
bag of bread;
I'll soon have this sorted out."

He ran over to where the baby
was holding his bag of bread
and not giving any to the birdies,
but eating it instead.

And he said, "What about some
for the ducky birds?"
But the baby started to…

scream!

So his brother said,
"If you let me hold the bag,
I'll let you hold my ice-cream."

Then the boy said,
"Quiet all you quack-quacks!
And stop pushing,
you're all going to get fed."
And he put his hand in the paper bag
and brought out a handful of bread.

So all the birds went quiet…

and the band stopped playing too…

And all the animals stopped making a noise,
including the animals in the zoo.

And suddenly the baby realized
they were all waiting for a crumb!
So he gave the ice-cream back
and he took a great big handful
of bread and...

threw!

all the ducky birds some.

Then all the hungry ducky birds
were ever so glad they'd come,
And instead of going…

honk! honk!
quacky quack-
quack!

all the birdies said…

MORE WALKER PAPERBACKS
For You to Enjoy

LITTLE SO-AND-SO AND THE DINOSAURS
by David Lloyd/Peter Cross

Little So-and-So is a very lively baby dinosaur.
He loves to run around and splash and shout and play silly games with the
other dinosaurs – under the watchful eye of his mother, So-So-Slowly.

"Bright, unusual paintings … full of fun and action …
beautifully produced." *Options*

0-7445-2029-0   £3.99

FINISH THE STORY, DAD
by Nicola Smee

Ruby is never happier than when her dad reads her a bedtime story.
But she hates it when he stops before the end … Ruby doesn't realize, though,
that her story is just beginning!

"Humorously moral … Nicola Smee tells a neat story, making her point
without preaching." *Julia Eccleshare, Children's Books of the Year*

0-7445-3038-5   £4.99

MRS POTTER'S PIG
by Phyllis Root/Russell Ayto

Everything in Mrs Potter's house is spotlessly clean – except for baby Ermajean.
She's always in a mess. "You'll turn into a pig someday," Mrs Potter warns her.
And, one day, she does!

"Toddlers and older children, amused by the mess babies make,
will enjoy this story." *The Observer*

0-7445-5262-1   £4.99

Walker Paperbacks are available from most booksellers, or by post from B.B.C.S., P.O. Box 941, Hull, North Humberside HU1 3YQ
24 hour telephone credit card line 01482 224626

To order, send: Title, author, ISBN number and price for each book ordered, your full name and address,
cheque or postal order payable to BBCS for the total amount and allow the following for postage and packing:
UK and BFPO: £1.00 for the first book, and 50p for each additional book to a maximum of £3.50.
Overseas and Eire: £2.00 for the first book, £1.00 for the second and 50p for each additional book.

Prices and availability are subject to change without notice.